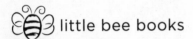 little bee books

An imprint of Bonnier Publishing USA
251 Park Avenue South, New York, NY 10010
Copyright © 2018 by Little Bee Books
All rights reserved, including the right of reproduction in whole or in part in any form.
Little Bee Books is a trademark of Bonnier Publishing USA, and associated colophon is a trademark of Bonnier Publishing USA.

Library of Congress Cataloging-in-Publication Data
Names: Reed, Melody, author. | Pépin, Émilie, illustrator.
Title: Scarlet's big break / by Melody Reed; illustrated by Émilie Pépin.
Description: First edition. | New York, NY: Little Bee Books, [2018]
Series: The Major Eights; #2 | Summary: The fame the Major Eights experience after the Battle of the Bands competition goes to Scarlet's head and she signs up for the school's talent show as a solo artist.
Identifiers: LCCN 2017039188 (print) | Subjects: | CYAC: Bands (Music)—Fiction. | Friendship—Fiction. | Talent shows—Fiction. | Loyalty—Fiction. | BISAC: JUVENILE FICTION / Readers / Chapter Books. | JUVENILE FICTION / Performing Arts / Music. | JUVENILE FICTION / Girls & Women. | Classification: LCC PZ7.1.R428 (print) | LCC PZ7.1.R428 Sc 2018 (ebook) | DDC | [Fic]—dc23
LC record available at https://lccn.loc.gov/2017039188

Printed in the United States of America LAK 1217
ISBN 978-1-4998-0568-0 (hc)
First Edition 10 9 8 7 6 5 4 3 2 1
ISBN 978-1-4998-0567-3 (pb)
First Edition 10 9 8 7 6 5 4 3 2 1
littlebeebooks.com
bonnierpublishingusa.com

THE MAJOR EIGHTS

SCARLET'S BIG BREAK

by Melody Reed

illustrated by Émilie Pépin

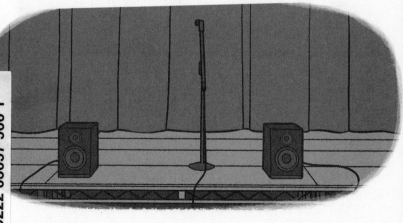

little bee books

CONTENTS

OH, SAY, CAN YOU SING?

It all began the week after the Battle of the Bands.

I was sitting in the bleachers on Saturday morning, watching my little brother Tyson's baseball game. Wind shook the leaves on the trees. I wished the sun would come out.

Then Coach Suarez walked over. "Scarlet, right?" she asked.

I jumped up. "What?"

1

"From the Major Eights? At the Battle of the Bands?" asked Coach Suarez.

Jasmine, Becca, Maggie, and I hadn't won the competition, but the crowd had loved us. We got an honorable mention. And we'd had a blast.

I blinked. "That's me."

"Do you know the national anthem?" she asked.

"Of course," I answered Coach Suarez. I looked over at Aunt Billie. She stood near my parents, watching Tyson. Aunt Billie lives just two blocks away from us. She's not only my aunt; she's also my singing coach. She grinned at me from the fence.

"Would you sing it this morning? To start the game?" Coach Suarez asked. "I just got a call. The woman who was going to sing for us today is sick."

My eyes bugged out. *"Really?"* Now I really jumped up. "You want me to sing? Here?"

"You girls did a great job last week," Coach Suarez said. "The whole town's talking about it."

When it comes to singing, nobody needs to ask me twice. "I'll do it!" I said. "Do you have a mic?"

"We have a PA system over here."

"Then let's do this!" I skipped down the bleachers.

And just like that, I had my first solo gig.

Coach Suarez left to prep the PA system.

Aunt Billie came over. "See?" she whispered. "The one song every singer needs to know. You never know when you'll need it." Aunt Billie was named after a famous singer. She is a singer, too. A really good one.

Coach Suarez passed me the mic. The crowd got quiet. Even the five-year-old ballplayers held still. We all turned to face the flag.

I started to sing. "Oh, say, can you see. . . ."

But then the mic cut out!

My eyes got big. I kept singing anyway. I acted like it was fine.

". . . By the dawn's early light. . . ."

The mic *still* didn't work. Wind blew across it, and it picked *that* up just fine.

But I kept on singing.

I paused after "ramparts." I'd had enough of this mic.

I set the mic down. I turned and faced the crowd and belted out the rest.

At ". . . la-and of the *FREE*," I was in the *zone*. People clapped and hooted. I finished the song: ". . . and the hooooome . . . of the . . . braaaaaaave!"

The crowd cheered.

Tyson pointed at me. He yelled, "That's my sister!"

Still clapping, Coach Suarez made a face. "Sorry about the microphone. You handled it great, though!"

"What a pro!" said a parent.

Coach Suarez dug in her purse. She handed me an orange piece of paper. "Have you heard about this?" she asked. "My kids go to your school. I saw this yesterday."

I read the flyer aloud:

ENTER THE TALENT SHOW!

BRING YOUR TUTUS.
BRING YOUR ROUTINES.
BRING YOUR VOICE!

A WEEK FROM FRIDAY, 7PM.
IN THE GYM. COME BE
A SUPERSTAR!

Wow.

A picture popped into my head. I was in the spotlight. I was singing at that talent show. And everybody in the whole school cheered! I grinned.

"Thanks," I said to Coach Suarez.

She squeezed my shoulder and left.

I hugged the flyer. Maybe I could sing alone, like my aunt. Maybe I could even win. Maybe . . .

Kids grabbed their gloves. They lined up. Coach Suarez ushered them out onto the field.

Maybe . . . maybe I could be a superstar!

TWO ORANGE FLYERS

By Monday, I couldn't *wait* to tell the other Major Eights. I was going to sing in the talent show. And I was going to win it! I brought the orange flyer to school.

But at recess, Maggie bounced up and down. She waved a piece of orange paper of her own. "Did you guys hear about the talent show?" she squealed.

"*Yes!*" said Becca. She bounced along with Maggie.

I felt like we were on a trampoline, and Maggie had just stolen my bounce.

"What talent show?" asked Jasmine.

Maggie pointed at my flyer. "Oh, you saw it, too, Scarlet!"

"Uh, yeah," I said.

"Here at school," Becca told Jasmine. I looked at my flyer.

There was writing on it in the bottom corner that I hadn't noticed before.

"Only forty spots," read Jasmine. "Sign up now!"

Becca studied the flyer. "We better sign up right away to get in!"

My eyes hit the bottom of the page. It was my turn to bounce up and down. I read it aloud. "The top three acts will perform at the Arts Banquet."

"That's a big deal!" Becca exclaimed. "My mom helps with the banquet every year. It's next month."

"What is it?" I asked.

"It's a fancy dinner," Becca said. "People pay a lot to go. It raises money for the school. For the arts and stuff."

"So, whoever wins gets to perform there, too?" I asked.

"Oh my gosh! Oh my gosh! Oh my gosh!" screamed Maggie. Her bouncing became jumping.

The picture in my head changed. I was still singing, but the audience wore nice dresses and tuxedos. My own dress was red and sparkly. It had that poufy stuff under the skirt. . . .

"Earth to Scarlet," Becca said.
"So, are you in?" Jasmine asked.
They all looked at me, waiting.

I couldn't stop thinking about the spotlight. "Oh, I'm *way* in."

"Oh good!" said Jasmine. "Let's sign up after school."

"But we all catch the bus right after school," Becca said.

"Not Scarlet. Her aunt picks her up," said Maggie. She turned to me. "Could you sign us up, Scarlet?"

Us? Uh-oh. I didn't want to hurt my friends' feelings, but I wanted to sing by myself. I swallowed. "Uh, sure?"

"Perfect!" said Jasmine.

"Great!" said Becca.

"EEEEEEE!" screamed Maggie.

I wasn't sure what was going on at first, but then I realized: I had just agreed to do the talent show with the band.

This was a very big problem.

3

CENTER STAGE CAFÉ

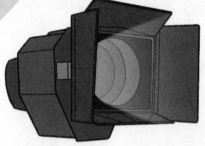

That night, I drew pictures on my homework paper.

I hadn't signed up for the talent show. I wanted to make my friends happy, and singing with them is fun. But I also wanted to sing by myself. I didn't know what to do.

There was no rush, though. I still had some time.

I doodled a dress on my paper and looked over to watch Aunt Billie sing.

Aunt Billie wore a silky black dress. She sang by herself in the middle of the stage. The spotlight made her hair shine.

Aunt Billie works at Center Stage Café. Whenever our parents work late, Tyson and I eat here, and I do my homework, too. Mom and Dad both work at the city hospital. They work nights sometimes, so we come to the café a lot. Everybody here is like one big family.

I felt a tug on my skirt. "What?" I whispered.

"Feed me," a voice growled under the table.

I rolled my eyes. Our baskets were empty. Ketchup clung to the wrapper on Tyson's. *Yuck!* I wouldn't touch ketchup if you *paid* me. "Tyson, you already ate your burger."

He poked his head out from under the table. His monster toys lay around him on the floor. He pulled down on his cheeks so his eyes looked gross. "Feeeeed meeeee."

Before I could argue, Tyson looked behind me. He shouted, "Kyle!"

The stage manager stood there. He grinned. He held another basket.

I shushed Tyson.

"Did I hear a monster growling for food?" Kyle whispered. He slid the basket onto my table.

"Fries!" Tyson said. He jumped into a chair. "Any ketchup?" he asked.

I wrinkled my nose.

Kyle didn't miss a beat. He placed a bottle onto the table.

"Just don't tell your aunt about the fries." Kyle winked. He saw my paper. "That's a pretty dress. What's it for?"

I shrugged. "The talent show."

"You don't sound happy about it," Kyle said.

"My friends want our band to enter. But I want to sing by myself. Like Aunt Billie."

"Ah," said Kyle. He picked up our empty baskets. "That band of yours is pretty good."

I nodded.

"Well, why not do both?" Kyle asked. He checked his watch. "Uh-oh! I've got to get backstage."

"Huh?" I asked. But Kyle was gone.

Wait—that was it! With *and* without the band! Why hadn't I thought of that before? All I had to do was enter the talent show twice. Once by myself. Once with the band. There were three winners, a fter all. Both of our acts could win! I could sing by myself at the banquet, *and* I could perform with my band there. It was perfect!

I would sign up myself and the Major Eights first thing in the morning.

THE LAST SPOT

I tapped my foot. I folded my arms. There were still eight kids in front of me in line.

The five-minute bell rang. Lots of kids behind me left the line. A few in front of me left, too. They ran to get to class. I tugged on my backpack straps while I waited.

A fifth-grader was in front of me. He told the teacher how great he was at magic. He said he could do a disappearing act.

I wished he would make himself disappear from the line.

He finally ran for class. It was my turn.

"Well," breathed Ms. Stockman, the teacher in charge of the talent show. "Our last spot! And what's your name, dear?"

Last spot?! "Uh . . . Scarlet. Scarlet Johnson." She scribbled my name down in the last box on the page. I gulped.

"Grade?" she asked.

"Third," I said.

"And what will you be doing?"

I paused. *Me?* Well, of course . . . "Singing."

"With anyone else?" she asked. "Or just you?"

I opened my mouth to answer. I meant to say, "With my band, the Major Eights." But I thought about singing at Tyson's ball game. I thought of my aunt, singing solos onstage at the café.

"Just me," I said. I swallowed down the lump of guilt in my throat. "Just . . . me."

⑤ A CAPELLA

For two days, I hid from the other Major Eights. It wasn't hard. We didn't have any band practices lined up until later in the week. And at school, we were all in different classes, so I don't always see them. But just to be safe, at recess, I volunteered to help my teacher organize our bookshelves.

Finally, it was the night of the dress rehearsal for the talent show.

I stood up onstage in the gym. It was my turn to practice what I was going to sing.

I shifted from foot to foot. The gym lights lit up the empty chairs. Kids practiced their acts in corners of the gym and backstage. Only a few people watched me.

Aunt Billie says I was born for the stage. I never get nervous.

But tonight, I was.

"Name?" Ms. Stockman asked.

The mic was too high. I stood on my toes. "Scarlet Johnson," I said.

She looked at her paper. "It says you'll be singing. What song?" she asked.

I'd decided to sing a song the band had been working on. It had a great lead vocal part. "Hold My Own," I said. "By the Silver Sporks."

"Okay, Scarlet. Do you have the music?"

My face fell. "Um . . . music?"

"Yes," Ms. Stockman said. "A CD? An audio file of some sort?"

I was so used to singing the song with the band, I'd forgotten all about musical backup! I swallowed. "Uh, no."

"So, you'll be singing *a cappella*," she said.

"Huh?"

"No music."

"Oh," I said. "Yeah." I sang the national anthem *a cappella*. I could do it with this song, too, right?

"Start whenever you're ready," said Ms. Stockman.

I waited for the guitar part. It's the beginning of the song. Then I remembered Becca wasn't there.

So, I started alone. "I've got to hooooold my ooooown . . ." I sang.

But I forgot to stand on my tiptoes to reach the mic. Jasmine always checks our mic heights before we start. The sound faded in and out during my singing.

In the middle of the song, I paused. This was where Maggie's drum solo went. She'd been working on it for weeks. I listened  to the solo in my head. I tried tapping my foot while I waited for it to end. I came back in, and finally finished the song.

I felt awful. This was one of my favorite songs to sing. It sounded so good when we played it together. By myself, it was a mess.

Ms. Stockman thanked me. I hurried off the stage.

I ran smack into Maggie. She looked like a melting snowman.

"I just checked the list," she said. "We're not on it. The show is full. What happened, Scarlet?"

"I mean, I tried," I said. "I got to the sign-up, and there were tons of kids in front of me. There was only one spot left."

Maggie's forehead scrunched up. "So, you *did* get us in?"

I realized my mistake too late. "Well, no . . ."

"You *didn't* sign us up," Maggie said, "but you signed *yourself* up."

Did she have to rub it in? "Well, like I said, there was only one spot left." I looked out the window at the line of cars picking kids up. "We'll get other gigs as a band. I have to go. My mom's waiting."

But when I turned to go, Becca and Jasmine were walking up to us. They looked worried.

"What happened?" asked Becca.

Maggie folded her arms across her chest.

It wasn't fair. I snapped. "Look, I saw the flyer first! I was already going to enter by myself!"

They blinked at me.

"I thought I'd sign us *both* up. You know, sing by myself *and* sing in the band." I took a deep breath. "But there was only one spot left. So . . . so, I took it." I looked down. "I'm sorry. I just really want to be a singer. Like my aunt."

I didn't wait to see their faces. I ran toward the cars.

I felt awful. But if I was going to be a real singer, I needed my big break. And singing at a fancy banquet could be that big break. *Anybody* could be in the crowd. A talent scout, even.

I didn't know what to do. I had no act. And now, I had no friends.

BAND PRACTICE

I flipped the light switch in the basement at Aunt Billie's house. Her recording studio lit up. When I need to cheer up, this is where I go.

I wandered around the room. I ran my fingers over the keyboard, the drum set, and the mixing board. I squished the gray foam on the walls. It keeps the good sounds in and the bad sounds out.

55

After last night, I had avoided the band again during the day at school. I knew they were mad, and I didn't really blame them.

I still had no backup music. I didn't play the keyboard. Or drums. Or guitar. I sighed. I would have to ask Aunt Billie if she had a backing track that could work.

"That was good, Scarlet," said Jasmine.

She, Becca, and Maggie stood on the stairs.

"Hey," I said, confused. "What are you guys doing here?"

Becca shrugged. "We haven't played together in a while. Your mom said you were down here."

I felt like singing the national anthem in the studio. Just to warm up. When I got to the hold note, I heard shuffling on the stairs. It was probably Tyson. He liked to be a monster and sneak up on people. I ignored him. But when I finished the song, I heard clapping.

"We get it," Jasmine said. "We know you wanted to be in the talent show by yourself. There weren't enough spots for the band, too."

"We'll have other gigs, like you told Maggie," said Jasmine. She nudged Maggie.

"Yeah," Maggie grumbled. She looked down at the floor.

"We know you need to practice," said Becca. "Do—do you want us to play something for you to sing along to?"

"Really?" I said, my eyes opening wide. "You'd do that? Even though we're not doing the talent show together?"

Jasmine shrugged. "Sure," she said. "Friends are more important than shows."

Becca nodded.

Maggie scowled at the floor.

"Um . . . I'd like that," I said.
"Thanks."

Becca skipped down the stairs. "Oh good!" she said. "I *love* playing down here."

Jasmine grinned. She skipped over to the keyboard.

Maggie sighed as she walked over to the drum set.

"Do you want to do the Silver Sporks song?" Jasmine asked.

Jasmine and Becca looked at me, waiting. But Maggie didn't. I realized she hadn't looked at me at all since the talent show rehearsal.

I swallowed.

"Okay," I said. "Let's do this!"

"One more, Scarlet!" called Kyle.

My arms shook, but I grabbed the last crate. I lugged it inside.

It was later that night. I felt better about my song now for the talent show. But something was bugging me.

When I pictured it, I still saw myself up onstage alone. But it didn't look fun anymore. It just looked ... lonely.

I dropped the crate at Kyle's feet.

He laughed. "You've got to take it up onstage, sweetie." I glared at him.

Tyson ran around the café. He growled through a monster mask. I felt a little jealous. But Kyle had asked for my help setting up for tonight, and that made me feel proud.

I finally set the box down on the stage. "Now what?" I asked Kyle.

He pointed. "Now I need a cable. It's black. It's in that box."

I went to the box. It was filled with black cables. I pulled one out and was surprised. Those cables were heavy! "This one?" I panted.

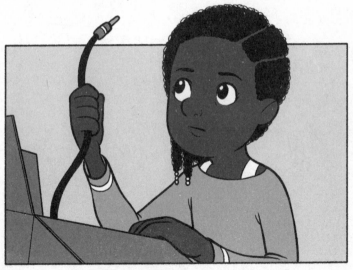

"That's it! Bring it over," said Kyle.

Kyle kept giving me tasks to do all night. After the cables were in the right places, we did a sound check. He showed me how to adjust the levels. Aunt Billie spoke into the mic, "Testing, testing." I brought the drummer her earplugs. I adjusted mic heights for the backup singers and then taped cables in place so no one would trip over them.

By the time the show started, I was pretty tired. I slumped into a chair next to Tyson. I watched Aunt Billie sing. The whole act looked different now. I still saw Aunt Billie in the spotlight. I still heard her awesome voice. But I also saw the backup musicians. My eyes followed all the cables. I turned and saw the sound guy behind us.

Kyle sat down next to me.

"I never knew how much work this is," I said. "So many people have to help out. I thought it was just about Aunt Billie."

He winked at me. "It takes a whole team, kiddo," he said.

Tyson perked up. "*I'm* on a team," he said.

I laughed. "We know, Ty," I said. "I just never realized Aunt Billie was, too."

And then I remembered *my* team.
I hadn't been a very good teammate
to them lately. I remembered them
helping me practice. And Maggie
trying to hide how upset she was.
They did all that for me.

And just like that, I knew what I
had to do. "Kyle!" I said. "Can I use
your phone?"

THE TALENT SHOW

Aunt Billie dropped me off at the gym. A banner read, "Talent Show—TONIGHT." I looked around. My friends weren't there yet. I bit my lip and went inside.

Backstage, girls in pink tutus twirled. Two rappers beat-boxed. A kid in a bear costume walked around. He kept bumping into people.

Becca, Jasmine, and Maggie were nowhere to be seen.

I stuck my head through the curtains to look into the auditorium, blocking the glare from the lights. Three judges shuffled papers at a table below the stage. I scanned the audience. No Major Eights there, either.

Ms. Stockman came up to me. "Scarlet, I got your message," she said. "Are your friends here?"

I swallowed. "Well, no. Not yet."

"Are you sure they're coming?" she asked.

"I left messages for them. I know they'll be here." But maybe they had changed their minds. Maybe Maggie had convinced them not to come.

"Well, let me know. You're up last, so there's still time." Ms. Stockman smiled and went to check on the other acts.

I sat on a bench by myself. The show started. Kid after kid went onstage. Then kid after kid came offstage. Finally, it was my turn.

Me. Just me. With no team.

The audience clapped for the act before me, the magician from the line the other day.

I swallowed the lump in my throat and smoothed down my dress.

Ms. Stockman motioned me over. A drum set, a keyboard, and mics were set up. But my friends were still not there. I stepped to the middle of the stage. The lights blinded me. I held on to the mic, hoping my hand would stop shaking.

"And now," said the announcer, "the famous Major Eights!" The audience cheered. The people present knew who we were. But the cheers died down when the curtain rose and the audience saw that there was only one Major Eight up onstage.

I waited for the music to start. Then I remembered I hadn't given the teacher any because I had hoped my band would show up. My eyes got big as I stared out at the crowd.

And I completely blanked.

I never blank. I love singing. I love crowds. But tonight, I could not remember the first words of the song.

⑨ HOLD MY OWN

Just when I was about to run offstage in embarrassment, I heard something. It started at the back of the gym. The audience turned toward it. I strained to see. It was a girl with a guitar, and the girl was coming closer. She was playing the opening chords of the Silver Sporks song.

It was Becca!

My face broke into a smile. And the words came back to me. I held the mic up and sang. "I've got to hold my own . . ."

Becca climbed the stairs to the stage and joined me, standing behind another microphone. We sang together, "but I can't do that all alone."

Behind us, someone started to play the keyboard. I whipped around. Jasmine smiled at me. Maggie sat behind the drums. She gave me a thumbs-up.

We all sang together, "I need you here with *me* . . . so I can be . . . who I was meant to *be*!" On the last "be," Maggie started her drum solo. I didn't have to count the beats anymore. She rocked the solo! When it was over, I knew when to start singing again.

We all sang the last part together. It was the best feeling ever!

When we finished, the crowd went wild. Everyone got to their feet, cheering and waving. I squinted. Mom, Dad, Tyson, and Aunt Billie all waved. Kyle had come, too.

Ms. Stockman came onstage. She whispered to us, "You girls gave me quite the scare. I thought you weren't coming."

"Sorry about that," said Becca. She turned to me. "We had trouble getting a ride. But then Maggie talked to her mom. She brought us in the minivan."

Maggie smiled at me. "Thanks for asking us, Scarlet. I know you really wanted to sing by yourself."

"Actually," I said, "I *thought* I did. But even a pro needs a team. Maybe I'll sing by myself one day. But for now, I want to sing with my friends. It's way more fun."

"Bring it in, everybody!" said Becca. She put her arms around us. We squished together for a group hug.

"I have the results," Ms. Stockman announced. The three judges beamed up at her from their table.

Becca, Maggie, Jasmine, and I linked our arms.

"As you know, the top three acts will perform at the Arts Banquet next month. This honor and the winner of the talent show goes to . . ." She studied her paper. "Edgar the Excellent!"

The magician kid ran out from backstage.

"Should we get off?" Maggie whispered. "What if we don't win?"

Becca wrinkled her brow. "She didn't tell us to leave."

"Maybe she forgot about us," Jasmine said.

Ms. Stockman kept reading. "And the second winning act is . . . Mrs. Heffner's first-grade class!"

Thirty pairs of tap shoes clattered out as excited children ran onstage. They blocked our exit.

"What do we do now?" Maggie whispered. "We're trapped!"

"Just keep smiling," I said. "Maybe no one will notice."

The teacher cleared her throat.

"And the final winning act is . . ." She paused. We held our breath. "Well, this one is no surprise. Center City's very own Major Eights!"

Maggie screamed. Becca jumped up and down. Jasmine hugged me. We were in! We were going to perform at the banquet!

And a new picture suddenly popped into my head. This time, *all* of us were in the spotlight.

We pulled in for another group hug. "We couldn't have done it without you, Scarlet!" said Jasmine.

I smiled back. "No, it took *all* of us,"
I said. "The Major Eights are a team."

"Always," said Maggie.

"Definitely," said Jasmine.

"Friends forever," said Becca.